W9-BGR-835

ITTY BITTY KITTY AND THE RAINY PLAY DAY

Joan Holub • Illustrated by James Burks

HARPER
An Imprint of HarperCollinsPublishers

For pretty, witty Tamar –J.H.

For Cinders and Sweetheart –J.B.

Itty Bitty Kitty and the Rainy Play Day

www.harpercollinschildrens.com

ISBN 978-0-06-232220-3

The artist used Photoshop CS5 with a Wacom Cintiq monitor to create the digital illustrations for this book.
Typography by Joe Merkel
15 16 17 18 19 SCP 10 9 8 7 6 5 4 3 2 1
❖
First Edition

ITTY BITTY KITTY

AND THE

RAINY PLAY DAY

It was a drippy-droppy, plippy-ploppy, rainy, gray, can't-play-outside day.

Which meant that Ava and
Itty Bitty Kitty were stuck *inside.*

Ava drew pictures on the foggy window.
Itty Bitty made pawprints.
And noseprints.
And whiskerprints.

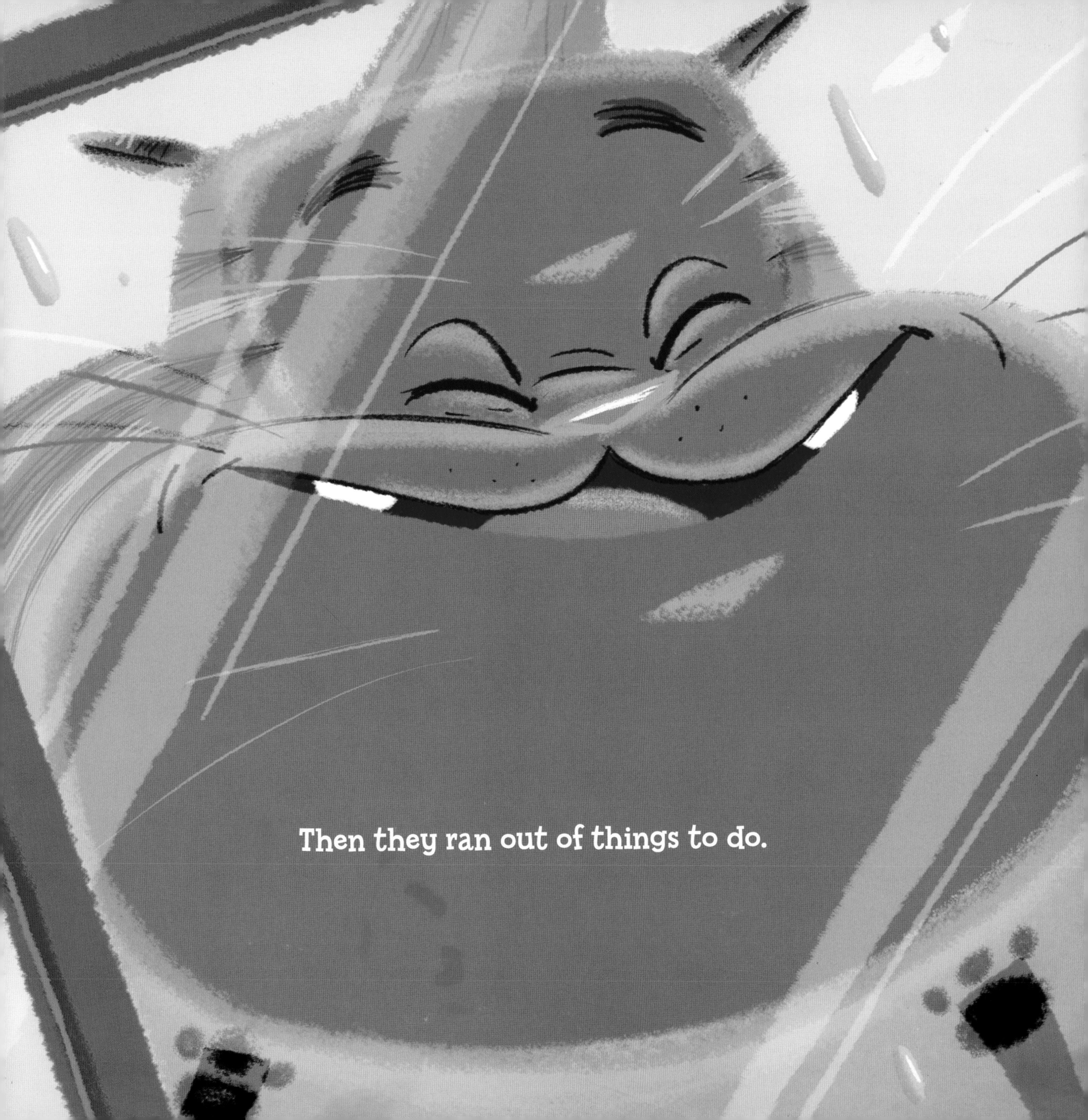

Then they ran out of things to do.

“When will the rain stop?” Ava asked Dad.
“Soon,” he told her.
“Soony balloony baboony,” grumped Ava.

"Turn that frown upside down," Mom told her.
"But there's nothing to do," said Ava.
"I know. Let's play a game called pick up your room," Mom suggested.

Ava and Itty Bitty didn't think that sounded fun, but they didn't have anything else to do . . .

…so Ava and Mom picked up her toys.
And Itty Bitty picked up her room.
It was hard work.

"We need a snack," Ava told her cat when they were done.

Together, they headed for . . .

... the kitchen.
Ava got her cup.
Itty Bitty got his dish.

Slurp! went Itty Bitty.
Burp! went Ava.

"That's enough of that," called Mom.
"Time for a different game."

So Ava and Itty Bitty
took off for . . .

. . . Dad's study.

"I know! Let's play Go Fish," said Ava.

But there was something an itty-bitty bit fishy about the way her cat played.

"Maybe cards are not your game," Ava told him.

Just then, Itty Bitty's left ear perked up.
In a flash, he dashed for . . .

...the living room,
where that cat jumped onto the cushy couch,
then onto the slightly unstable table,
then onto the wide windowsill.

Ava jumped onto the cushy couch,
then stepped onto the slightly unstable table,
then onto the wide windowsill, too.
"Whoever touches the floor is a rotten egg!" she yelled.

Itty Bitty bounced back to the cushy couch.
So Ava bounced back to the cushy couch.

They hopped from there
to the flowered red chair

to the footstool, where
that cat stopped to stare . . .

...at a little fish
on a high, high shelf.
Itty Bitty twitched.
His tail flicked. His whiskers wiggled.
He wanted that fish, like the one on his dish.

"MEE-OWWW?

he called to it.

But it wouldn't come down.
So he went...

...UP!

Itty Bitty leaped over the chair high into the air.
All paws and claws, he swung for that fish.

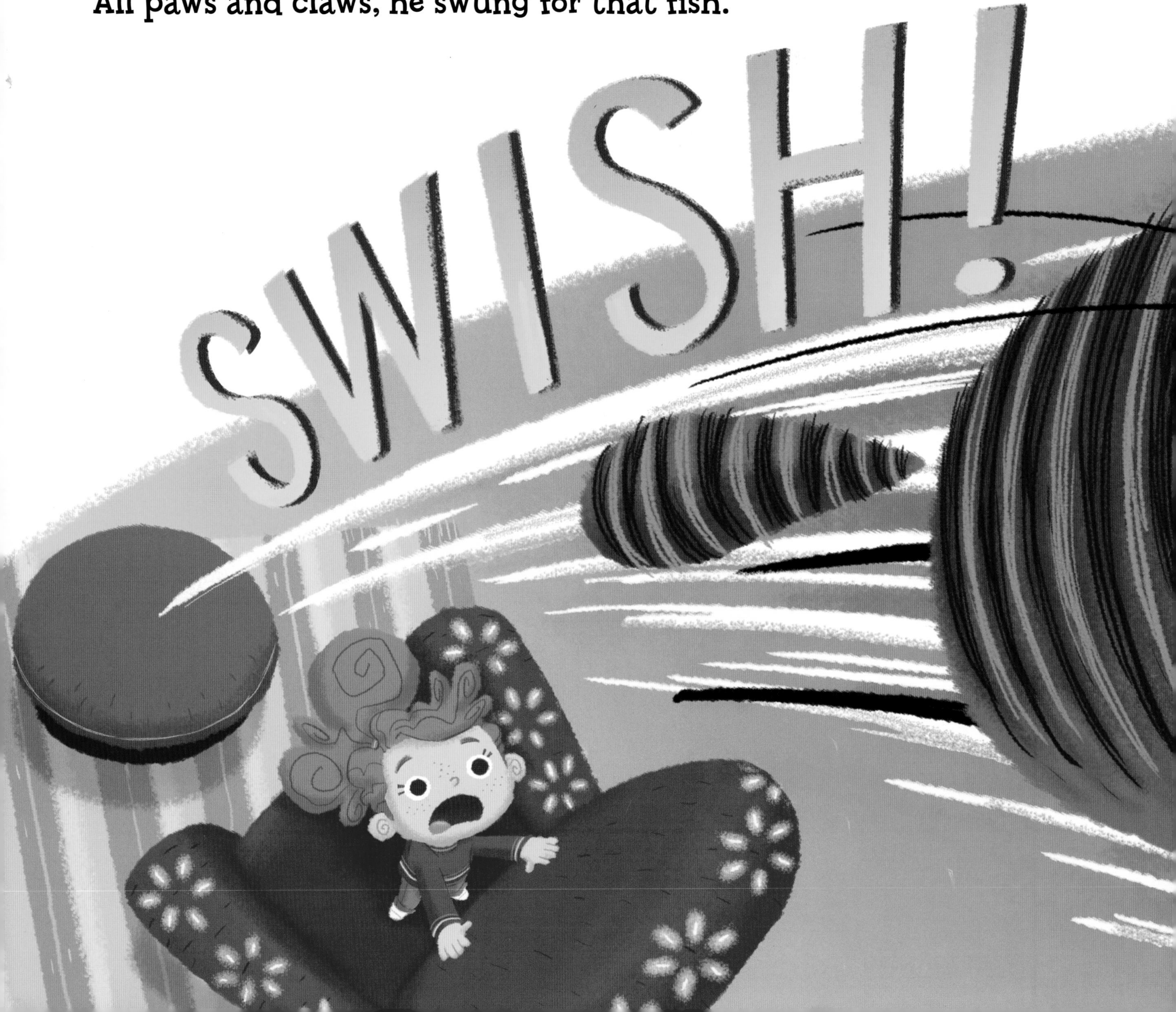

He didn't quite make it.
And that fish?
He *did* break it.

Just then, the sun peeked from the clouds.
"Out you go, you two," said Dad.
Ava and Itty Bitty hurry-scurried through the door.

But halfway down the path,
Itty Bitty froze in his tracks.
Then he turned, wild-eyed, and ran back inside!

Because it turned out that kitty was not one bit fond of wet-puddle paws!

So while Ava played outside,
Itty Bitty stayed inside.

Then Ava got a tremendous,
stupendous idea!
She zipped back into the house.

Minutes later,
Ava and Itty Bitty
dashed out again.
SPLISH!
SPLASH!

OOPS!

Oh, Itty Bitty!

But then everyone began to laugh.

Even the rainbow smiled.

Which was pawsitively purrfect.